Text copyright © 2009
by Candace Whitman
Illustrations copyright © 2009
by Steve Wilson
CIP Data is available.
Published in the
United States 2009 by
 Blue Apple Books
515 Valley Street
Maplewood, NJ 07040
www.blueapplebooks.com

Distributed in the U.S.
by Chronicle Books
First Edition
Printed in China

ISBN: 978-1-934706-54-1

10 9 8 7 6 5 4 3 2 1

lines that wiggle

by **candace whitman**

illustrations by **steve wilson**

blue apple books

lines that *wiggle*

lines that *bend*

wavy lines

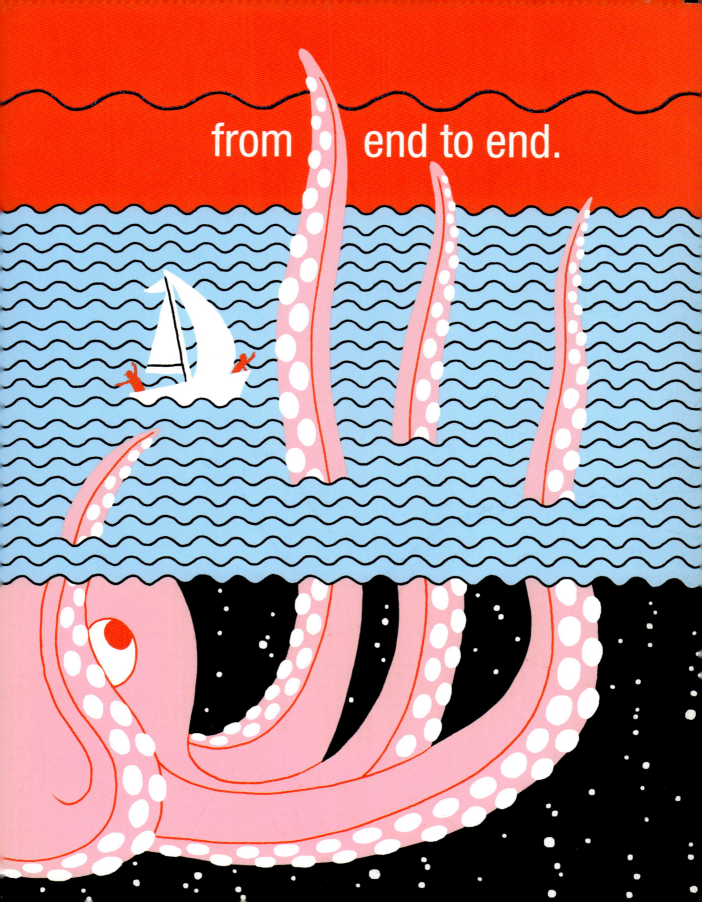

from end to end.

lines that
tickle

lines to *trap*

lines to *hide*

two lines running
side by side.

lines that
curve

lines that *curl*

underwater
lines that *swirl*.

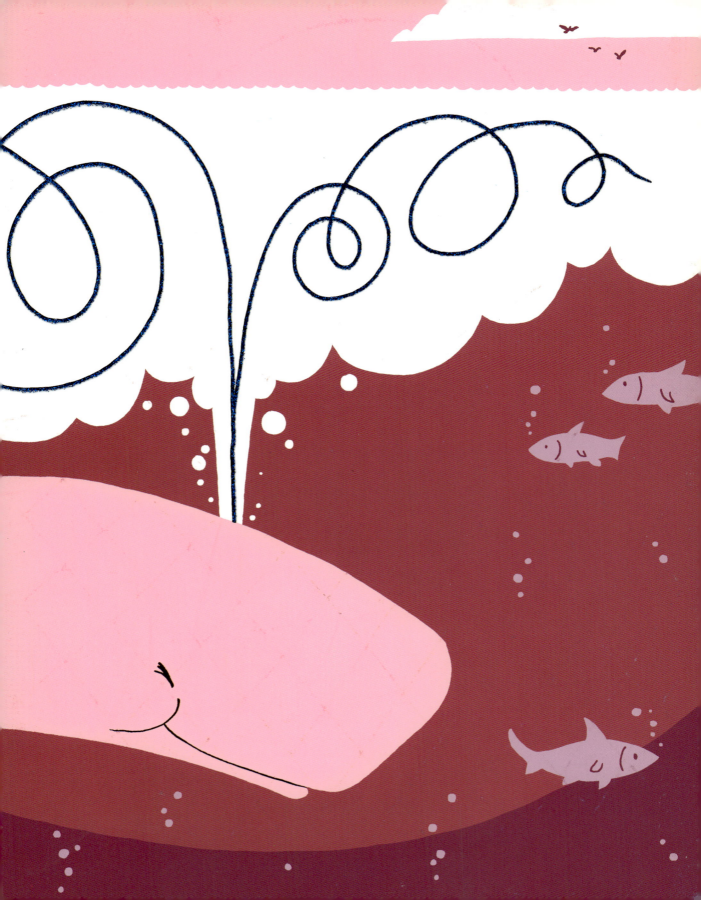

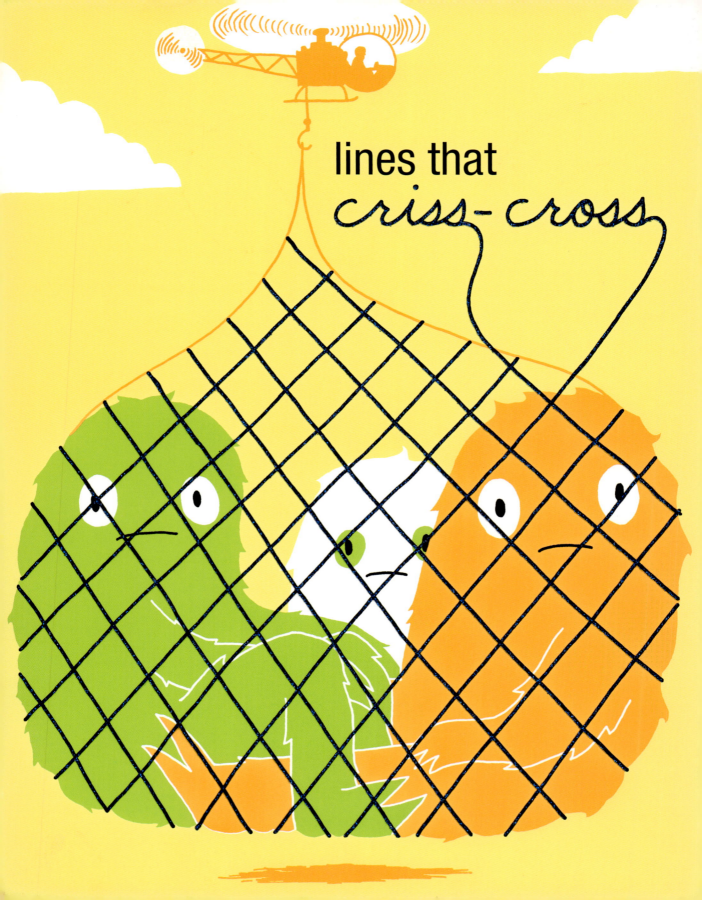

lines that mend

lines
with doggies at the end.

lines that
scurry

lines in

lines in leaves
that grow on *trees*.

lines that *twist*

lines that *sway*

lines that *swish* the flies away.

rainbow lines are way up high.

so find some *lines*
not in this book!